To all children:
Hold on to your dreams.

Library of Congress Cataloging in Publication Data.   Tallon, Robert. The alligator's song.
SUMMARY: Eddie helps a travel-weary alligator after hearing his melancholy song.
1. Alligators — Fiction. 2. Friendship — Fiction I. Title. PZ7.T157A1 E 80 – 19522
ISBN 0 – 8193 – 1043 – 3 ISBN 0 – 8193 – 1044 – 1 (lib. bdg.)

The Alligator's Song

ROBERT TALLON

PARENTS MAGAZINE PRESS · NEW YORK

Lightning flashed, thunder boomed,
and the wind howled.
Eddie jumped out of bed to close the window.

He couldn't believe what he saw in the garden.
A sad alligator was singing a song:

Please help me get down to the sea.
From there I'll swim back home.
I'm tired of travel.
No more will I roam.
Please help me get down to the sea.

"Ma, Ma!" shouted Eddie.
"There's an alligator outside my window.
Come look! Quick!"

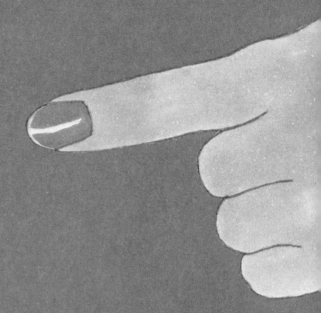

"Now go back to bed," she said.
"There is no alligator.
You've been reading that scary book again."

So Eddie went back to sleep.

Next day at school,
the alligator was outside the window.

"See you tonight," he said to Eddie.

That night, Eddie climbed a tree in his garden
and waited for the alligator.
Soon the alligator came strolling by.

Eddie slipped down from the tree
and followed him.
The alligator winked at Eddie.

Then tears began to drip from his eyes,
and he sang Eddie his sad song.

When I was little and lived at home.
I once went out on the beach alone.
A sailor took me to his ship,
and we set out on an ocean trip.

I liked to travel well enough,
except on days when the sea was rough.
But then I grew tired of life at sea,
and longed to be home with my family.

One day, the sailor brought me to town.
I fell from his knapsack onto the ground.
I thought I'd swim home to my family.
But try as I might, I could not find the sea.
Lonely and lost and shaking with fear,
I hid in these woods for almost a year.

Please help me get down to the sea.
From there I'll swim back home.
I'm tired of travel.
No more will I roam.
Please help me get down to the sea.

"I'll help you," said Eddie.
"Please, no more tears.
Tomorrow morning you'll be on your way."

The alligator was so happy,
he wanted to celebrate.
He asked Eddie to jump on his back
and carried him off up a steep hill.
They danced and played until the sun came up.
Then they headed for Eddie's house.

Eddie told the alligator to
climb into his red wagon.
Then he covered the alligator
with an old coat of his Dad's.
The wagon looked like a new kind of boat.

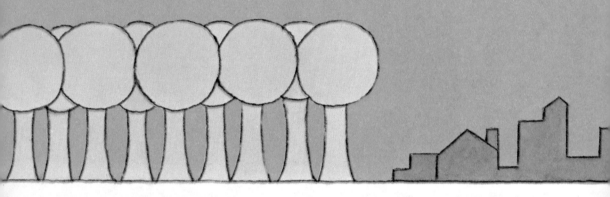

They walked and walked —
through the woods,
through the town,
down to the beach.

The beach was crowded.
Eddie said to the alligator,
"We'll never reach the water THIS way.
You'd better come out from
under that coat."

When people spotted the alligator,
they quickly cleared a wide path.

Eddie and the alligator
walked along waving to the crowd.

When they reached the water,
the alligator thanked Eddie
and gave him a present —
one of his teeth on a chain.
"Wear it, my friend," he said.
"It will bring you much happiness."

The alligator said good-bye and
thank you again,
and he swam out far to sea.

As Eddie pulled his empty wagon home,
he felt very sad.
But he was happy, too —
that his friend was
finally on his way home.

That night, when Eddie
was getting ready for bed,
he heard a noise at his window.
He couldn't believe what he saw.
A big white elephant was standing
in the garden.

"I want to leave for the jungle tonight,"
said the elephant.
"Please help me find my way."

"Ma, Ma!" Eddie shouted.
"There's a big white elephant
outside my window!
Come look! Quick!"

"Go back to bed," she said,
"and stop reading that scary book!"